Written and illustrated by
WJ Walton

Edited by
Joy Henley, Inkstained Editing

ISBN 978-0-615-79808-0

This book is a product of Awkward Labs
www.awkwardlabs.com
Pursue happiness - Follow your bliss

Please read this book aloud to someone else.
(Doing the voices is optional, but recommended.)

To all of my family and friends
who told me that this was possible.

You were right.

One evening,
when the sky was
bright,
and the water was
warm...

...a tiny creature pushed and pushed and hatched from a tiny egg.

6

Her name was Polly.

The very first thing that Polly felt was the movement of the water as it gently rocked her to and fro. She wiggled her legs back and forth, and soon discovered that doing this helped her move through the water. This was the very first thing that she learned.

The water was much stronger than her legs, however, and it carried her back and forth many times before she landed gently on a pile of bright, shiny eggs.

They were eggs that were just like the one she had just hatched from. Polly looked inside and saw a tiny creature just like herself inside of each of them.

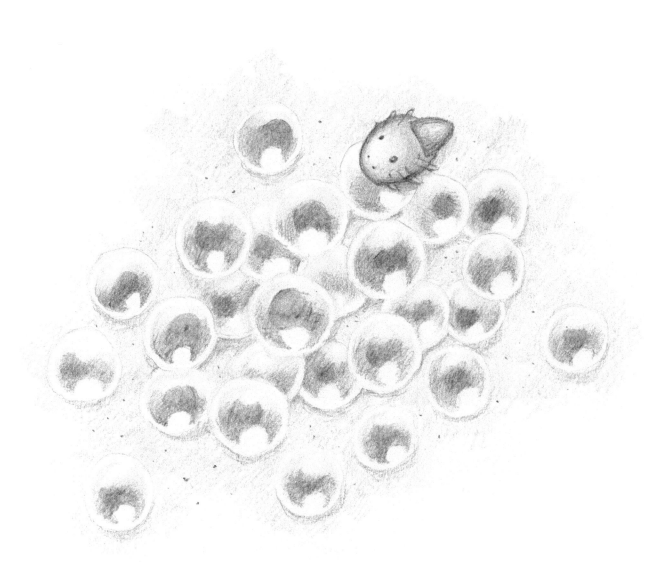

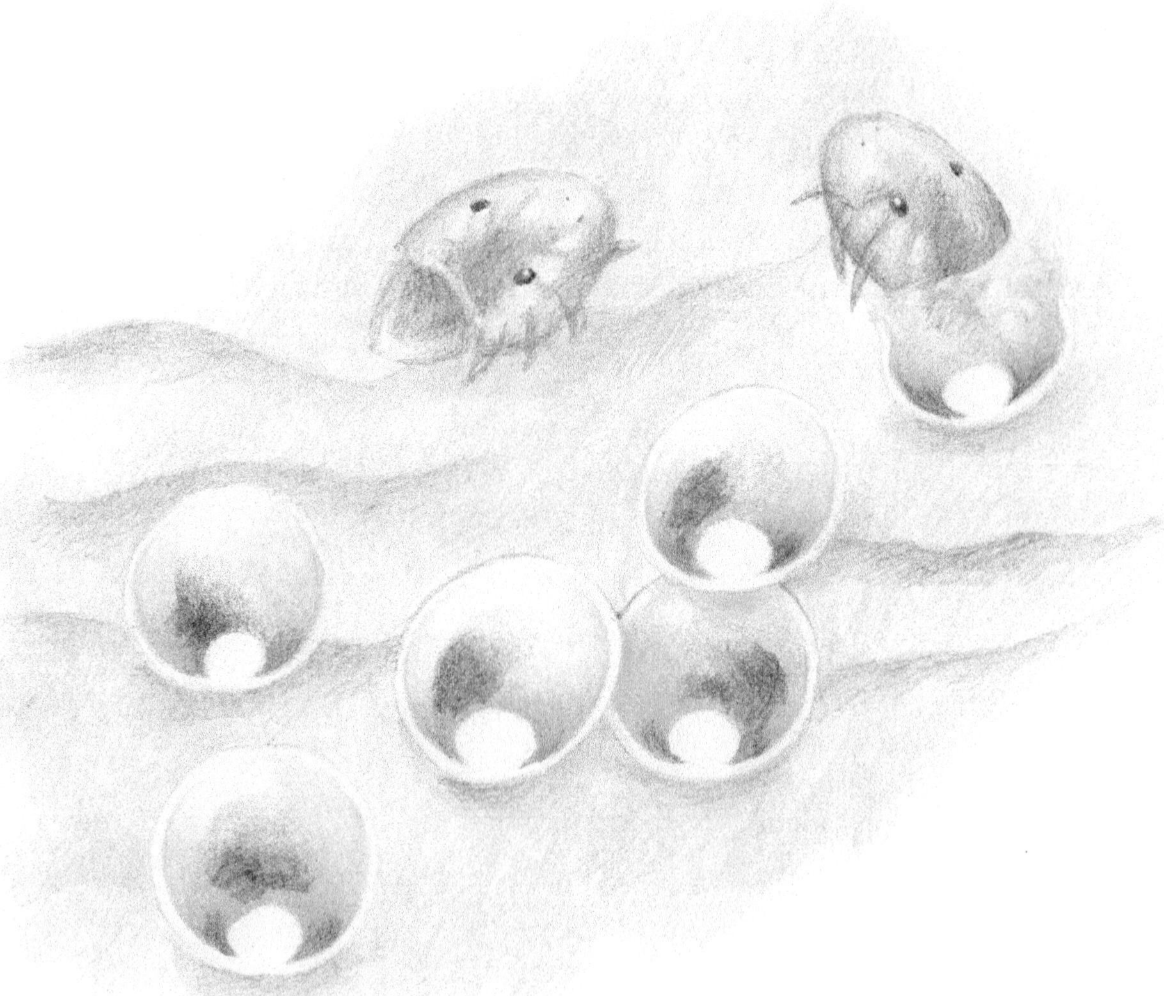

As she watched, one of the tiny creatures kicked and kicked and hatched from his tiny egg.

"Hello!" said Polly, but the water carried him away before he could answer.

Polly watched as more of the tiny eggs hatched, and tiny creatures like herself swam out of them and were carried about by the waves. In a moment, the waves carried her away as well, and washed her onto the shore.

And that is where she saw the most incredible thing she had seen so far:

...a dark sky filled with beautiful, shining lights.

"What are all of those beautiful lights?" she asked the others as they drifted by her. But none of them knew the answer to her question.

Polly admired the lights
until the sky slowly grew bright,
the lights faded, and a much bigger, brighter light rose in the sky.

Polly was amazed. She had to know more. But before she could watch for much longer, the tide swept her and the others from the shore and out into the deep sea.

There were lots of wonderful things to see and discover in her new home, but Polly couldn't stop thinking about the lights above. She asked some of the other creatures about them, but few of them knew very much, and all of them warned her about trying to see them again.

"You're too small!" Peg warned as she tapped on Polly's shell. "You'll get eaten too easily! Besides, you belong down here!"

But Polly could not resist. Whenever she had the chance, she would swim to the surface to have a look at the lights in the sky. She never stayed long, for fear that she might get eaten. Sometimes she would stretch some of her legs into the air to see if she could reach them.

Time passed, and as she grew, she shed her old tan shell for a new one that was green. Now she was large enough to take longer trips to the surface to see the lights in the sky. She even became brave enough to crawl up onto the sand and view the lights from there.

And one day, as she was doing this, she discovered something else that was incredible.

There were strange creatures all over the sand!

They were tall, and walked on only two legs, and
didn't appear to have any fins or gills or shells.
Their claws looked very strange, but they seemed
to be able to do lots of things with them.

"What are they?" she wondered aloud. She thought she was alone, but Ella and Squeak had just landed next to her, and thought she was talking to them.

"They're the Two-Feet-No-Wings!" said Ella.

"Squeak!" squeaked Squeak.

"Where do they come from?" asked Polly.

"Somewhere else," said Ella. "They like to come here when the sky is bright and the air is warm."

"Squeak!" squeaked Squeak.

Polly wanted to watch longer, but she knew that she couldn't stay out of the water for long when it was warm. So she crawled back into the water, eager to tell the others about her discovery.
The others already knew about them, however.

"The Two Feet? Stay away from them!" said Brock. "They are wild and unpredictable! You never know what one will do to you once they catch you!"

"They didn't seem so bad," said Polly.

"They used to do terrible things to your kind," said Brock. "They would smash your shells or leave you out of the water to dry out! And no one has ever understood why.

"If you're smart, you'll stay away from them, Polly!"

Polly wanted to be smart. But she also wanted to learn more about the Two Feet.

So she snuck away every chance that she could to observe them some more.

She saw some that made fascinating sounds...

...and some that were very quiet.

...some that were very active...

...and some that were quite still.

She learned everything that she could by watching the ways that the Two Feet behaved. She even learned a little bit about what they liked to eat.

And by watching them carefully, Polly learned that, when the air grew cold, the Two Feet didn't visit the shore as often...

...but when the air grew warm again, they always came back!

As time went on, and the days of warm and cold took their turns, Polly grew even more, and her new shell was darker. But she never lost her interest in the Two Feet.

One warm day, as she was watching the Two Feet on the beach, she was caught by surprise—a pair of them seemed to notice her, and walked over to her for a closer look!

Polly was scared and nervous and excited all at the same time. She wasn't sure what the Two Feet were going to do to her, so she sat as still as she could.

As they got closer, Polly noticed that one of the Two Feet was much smaller than the other. She guessed that it may have hatched not long ago.

"What is it, mama?" the small one said to the large one.

"Just leave it alone. It might be dangerous," replied the large one.

"It sure is ugly!" said the small one, and both of them walked away.

Polly understood most of what the Two Feet had said, but she didn't know what an "ugly" was.

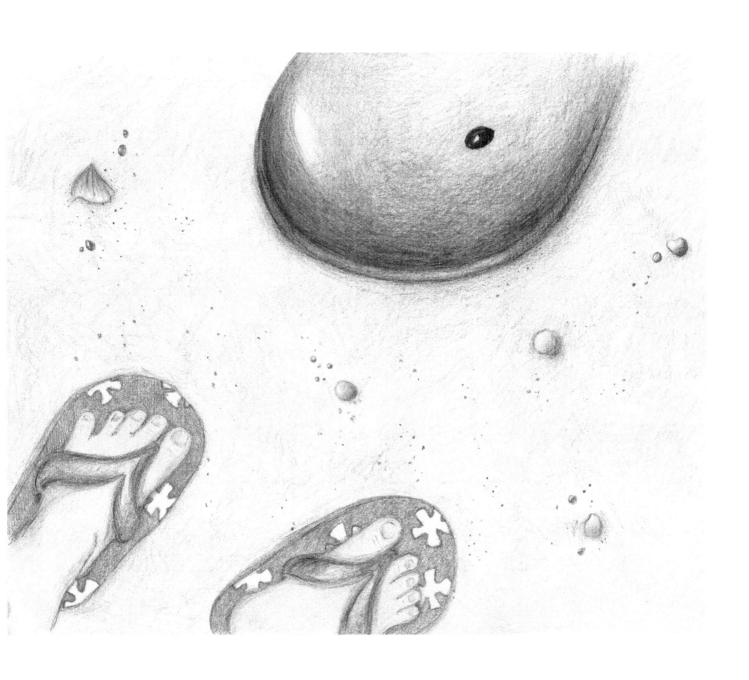

She asked Larry, who had just strolled up next to her.

"A Two Feet called me that when I stole some of their food," Larry said. "I think it means someone who is really good at stealing food!"

Polly hadn't stolen anyone's food, so she was pretty sure that wasn't it. So she asked some of the other creatures in the sea.

Del didn't know, and couldn't stop laughing about how silly the Two Feet look when they swim.

And all that Ang wanted to do was tell silly jokes.

"What did one ocean say to the other ocean?"

"I don't know," said Polly, "I was just wondering if you knew anything about—"

"Nothing! They just waved! Hah? Hah? Good one, right?"

"Yes," said Polly. "I'm sorry, but I really have to go."

Finally, she asked Peg, who didn't know the answer, but knew where to find it.

"The only way to find out is to ask one of the Great Wise Ones."

"Who are they?" asked Polly.

Peg told Polly that the Great Wise Ones were the oldest and wisest creatures in the sea, and that they knew everything that there is to know. "Only the wisest of all get to be a Great Wise One, and they live in the deepest, darkest part of the ocean."

Polly tried very hard to pay attention to the rest of what Peg was telling her, but she couldn't help wondering what the Great Wise Ones were like. Were they scary? Were they kind? How far would she have to go to see one? Would it be dangerous?

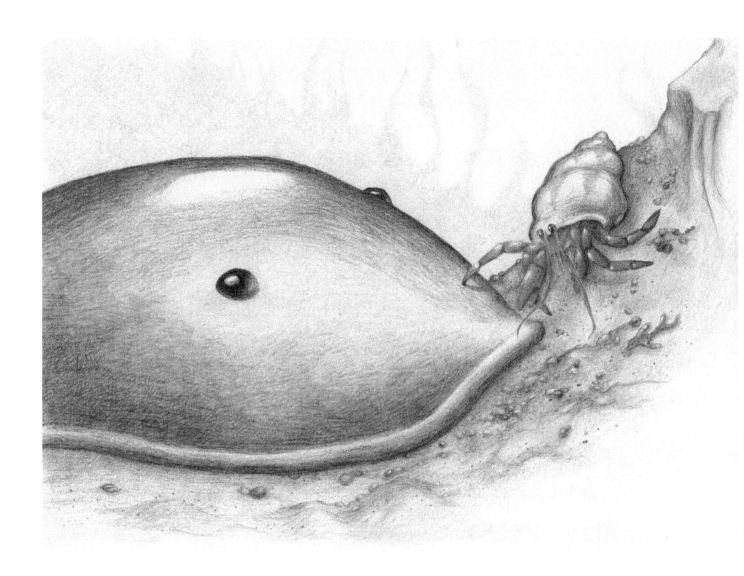

"Are you paying attention?" shouted Peg, who was tapping angrily on Polly's shell. "I said you're going to have to take them an offering!"

"What kind of an offering?" asked Polly.

"Something rare and precious. The Great Wise Ones don't share their knowledge without an offering!"

Polly thanked Peg for her help, and swam off to find something to give as an offering.

After a little bit of searching, she found the perfect thing—a shiny shard, worn smooth by the sand. It was as blue as the sky when the great light was shining, and Polly knew from her observations that it came from the Two Feet.

So she caught it up in her claws, tucked it snugly under her shell, and swam off in search of one of the Great Wise Ones.

She swam and swam, deeper and deeper, into the darkest part of the ocean, with the precious piece clutched tightly under her shell.

Many times she thought she had reached the very bottom of the ocean floor, but found that she could go even deeper.

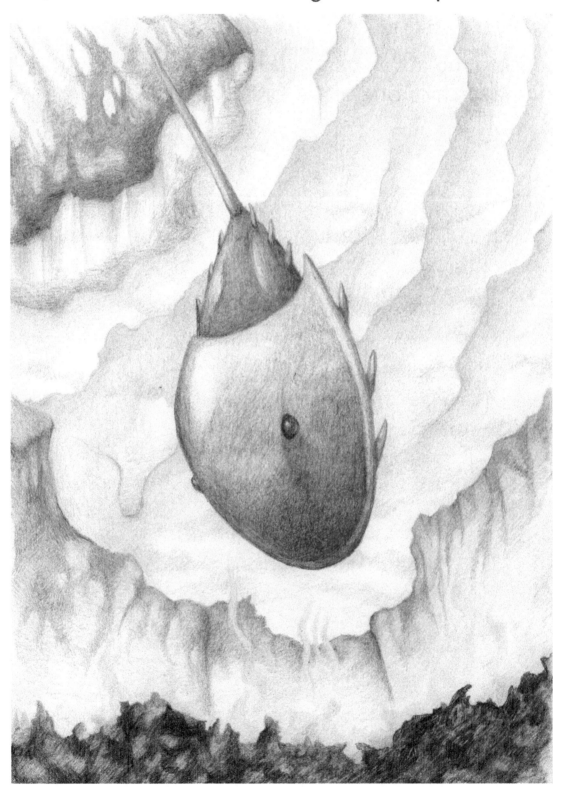

After a long, long time, she came to a place where the water grew darker than she had ever seen it before, and shadowy shapes shifted all around her. Her legs and gills were very tired, and she hoped that she was nearly there.

It was then that she heard a voice, deep and loud, but friendly-sounding, call out to her. "Come forward, Ancient and Unchanging One!" it said.

Polly could barely see through the shadowy shapes, but she could sense that there was nothing to be afraid of, so she swam forward. As she did, she looked all around, hoping to catch a glimpse of the Great Wise One.

"Why did you call me that?" she asked.

"Because your kind has remained unchanged for longer than any other citizen of the sea," said the Great Wise One. "And that includes myself!"

As he spoke, Polly began to see brief glimpses of him through the shadowy water.

He was so large that she couldn't see all of him at once—but she could tell that he had very large eyes and lots of legs.

"What brings you to my part of the water, Ancient One?"

"I have a question for you, and I was told that you were the only one who would know the answer."

"Is that so? Well, I suppose we will see about that. What is your question, Ancient One?"

Polly wasn't sure how to put it. So she decided to tell him the whole story.

"I've been watching the Two Feet a lot lately, because… well, I'm just very curious about them. And one day I heard one of them say that I was an Ugly. Can you tell me what an Ugly is?"

The Great Wise One was quiet for a moment, and Polly imagined that he was thinking about her question. Finally, he spoke.

"Ugly? Hmmm. I'm not sure I know that word. One of the Two Feet used it, you say?"

"Yes," said Polly.

"No, I'm sorry. I don't know what that word means. We don't use that word here in the ocean."

Polly was very disappointed.

"But I thought the Great Wise Ones knew everything there is to know! That's what Peg told me, anyway!"

"Oh, no. On the contrary," he replied, "the first step to becoming a wise one is knowing that you do not know everything."

Polly wasn't very happy with not having her question answered, and the Great Wise One could sense it.

"Sometimes, we have to accept that some of our questions will never be answered," he said. "Do you have any other questions for me, perhaps?"

Polly started to say that she didn't, and then realized that she did. "I'm very curious about the Two Feet and I want to learn all that I can about them. But the others tell me that this is dangerous and wrong. Are they right?"

"Ah, you *are* a curious one!" he told her. "You must be, or you wouldn't be here, would you? I'm sure that you know the answer to this question already, but there are times when we need to hear it from others before we believe it.

"There is nothing wrong with learning about those things that fascinate you, and what you learn may even help you and others in ways that you never thought of. In fact, the Two Feet themselves do it all of the time!"

"They *do?*" Polly asked.

"Of course! The Two Feet are very curious creatures. They are always exploring our home, and examining things that they find here. They must still have much to learn, because they frequently come back to learn more. They have even been trying to find me for ages, but I'm very good at hiding.

"So to you, Ancient and Unchanging One, I say carry on with your curiosity for as long as it makes you happy."

That made Polly feel a lot better. The Great Wise One was right—learning was a good thing. She already knew this, but had been hoping to hear it from someone else.

"If it's all right, may I ask another question?" she said quietly. She wasn't sure how many questions she was allowed to ask.

"Oh, please do!" said the Great Wise One.

"It's about the lights in the sky. When the great light is gone, you can see so many smaller lights in the dark. What are they?"

The Great Wise One's voice grew hushed and excited. "I am so glad that you asked! That is a subject that I have been studying for a very long time now!

"I'm not certain yet, but if my ideas are correct, those smaller lights are really many more great lights like our own, but much, much further away."

Polly thought about this for a moment, and all sorts of wonderings began to swarm in her brain. "Does that mean that there are others of my kind there? And yours? And Two Feet, too?"

"Perhaps. But I cannot be certain. And I will probably never know for sure," he said, a little sadly. "And I must accept that it's a question that will never have an answer."

Polly understood perfectly.

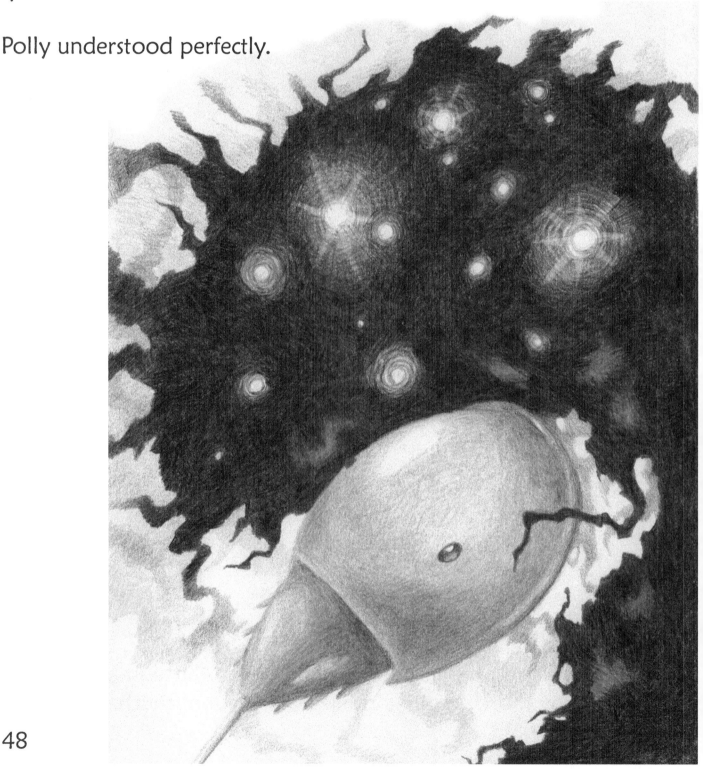

"Ancient One, there is one thing that you must remember, no matter what. Every one of us has a responsibility to our kind, and it is very important that we see to it. It is good to learn all that you can about the things that interest you and find happiness in that way, but you must never forget to take the time to fulfill your responsibility!"

"My responsibility? What do I have to do?" asked Polly.

"You will understand, Ancient One, when the time is right."

Polly wanted to inquire more, but didn't want to be a nuisance.

"Thank you for your time, Great Wise One," she said. "I really should go now." She started to swim away, but then stopped.

"Oh! I almost forgot your offering!"

"Offering?" he asked.

"Peg told me that I had to give you an offering in return for your knowledge."

She pulled the precious piece out from under her shell and held it out in one of her little claws.

"The Great Wise Ones do not require offerings in return for our knowledge. It wouldn't be right. But I can see that you chose this with great care, and carried it safely for such a great distance. I will keep it as a reminder of your visit."

Polly told the Great Wise One goodbye, but not before she promised him that she would return on another day to share with him some of what she had learned.

Time passed, and Polly grew older, but she never stopped exploring and learning.

Her travels took her from one end of the oceans...

...to the other.

She learned everything that she could about everything that she saw. But her favorite subject of all was always the Two Feet.

And she made frequent visits to her friend the Great Wise One, to share the things she had learned.

Sometimes, she even taught him something!

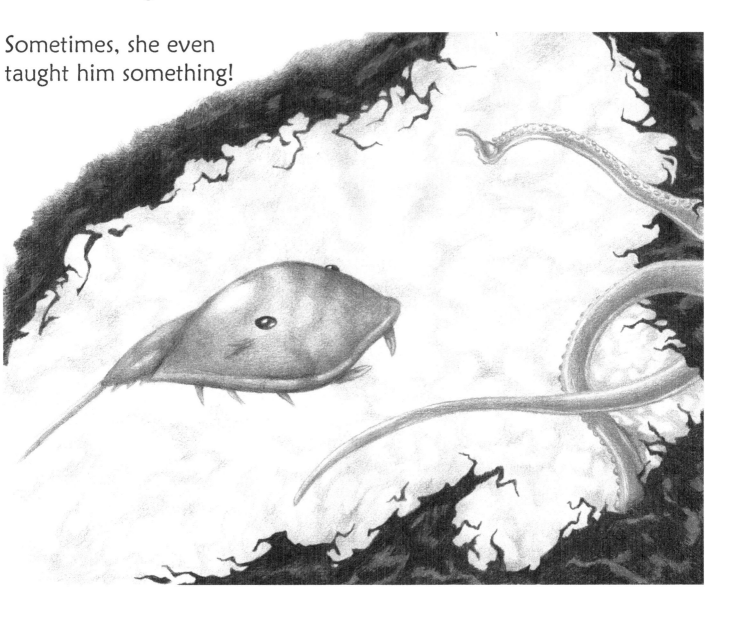

As the seasons went by, Polly grew even older. Her shell collected scuffs and cracks from her many adventures, and other creatures began to make their own homes on it.

She knew that it would not be long before she could no longer explore the way that she used to. So she took one last trip above the waves, to look at the lights one final time.

Once she left the water, she noticed a group of other creatures of her kind crawling around on the sand in wide loops and circles. Instantly, she remembered what the Great Wise One had said about her responsibility to her kind, and now she knew what it meant, and what she had to do.

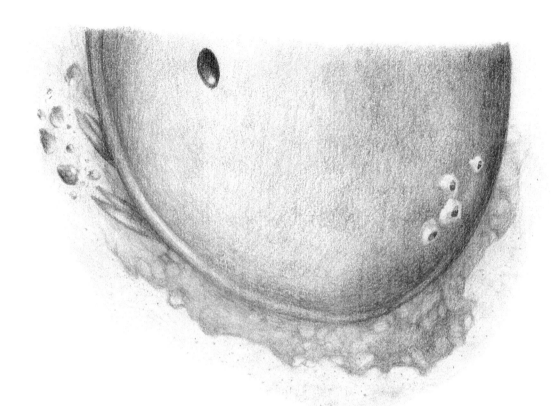

She crawled out onto the sand with the others, found a spot that seemed to be right, and began to dig a hole. Once it was deep enough, she positioned herself over it and laid her eggs.

Another one of her kind, a male, was clinging tightly to the back of Polly's shell, and as she dragged him over the eggs, he fertilized them, because this was his responsibility.

When both of them were finished, Polly looked down into the hole at the eggs she had laid, and saw that they shone just like the lights in the sky.

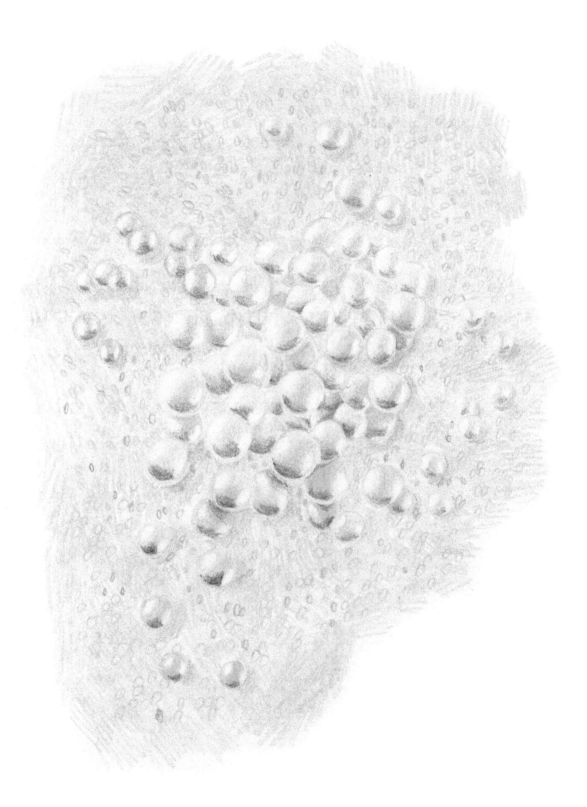

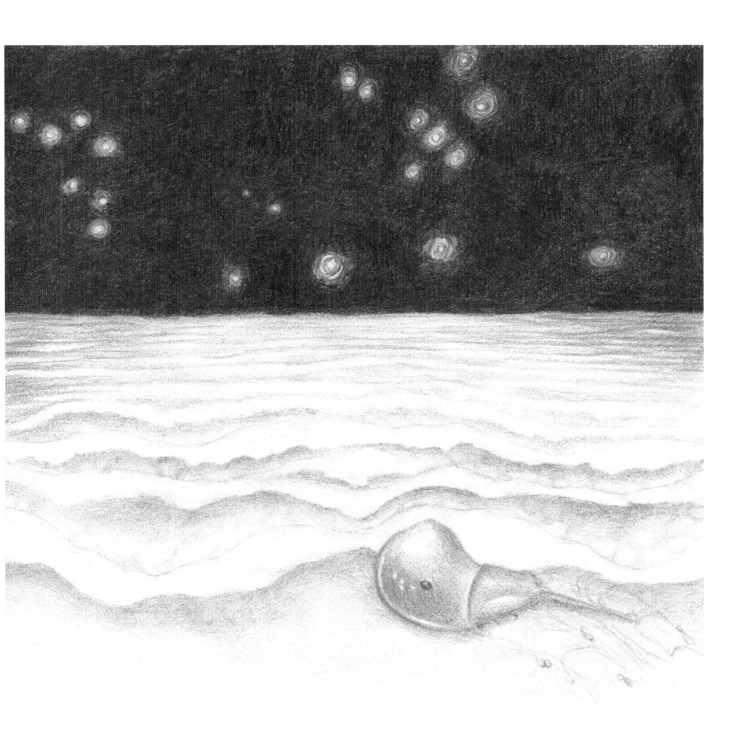

Then Polly crawled back to the ocean, taking one last look at the lights before the waves covered her.

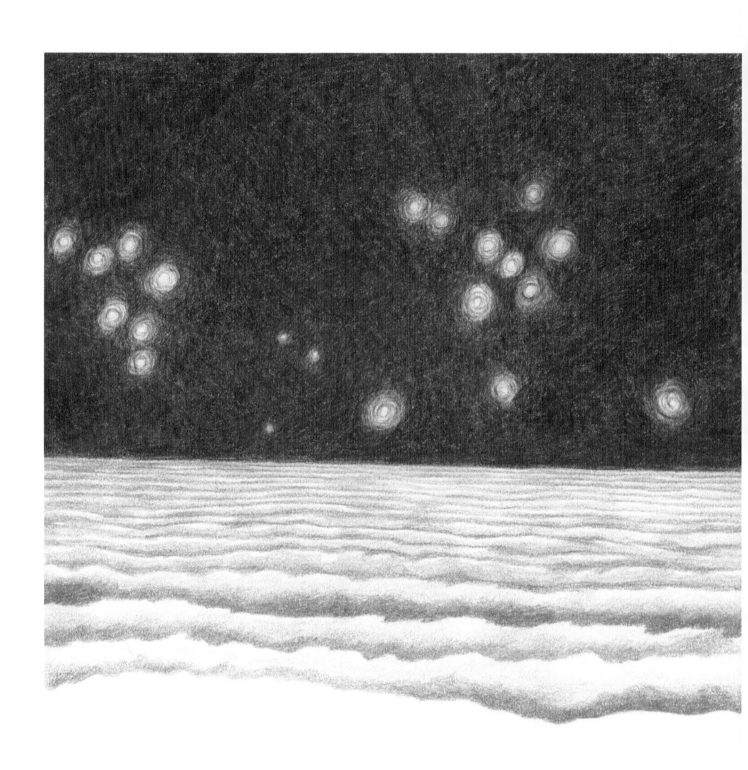

One evening, when the sky was bright and the water was warm, a tiny creature kicked and kicked and hatched from a tiny egg.

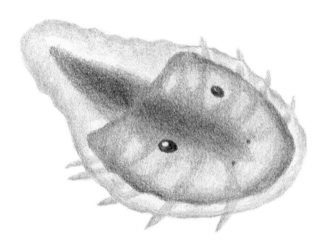

His name was Carl.

Carl was very curious and inquisitive. As he grew, he discovered many things that he wanted to learn more about, and he was always exploring, sometimes in places where he was not welcome. He constantly asked questions, and questions about the answers to the questions, and questions about those answers, as well.

He wanted to know why water fell from the sky sometimes and what the strange creatures on the beach were called and why Molly lived in such a small house and if she ever felt cramped in there, and a whole lot of other things.

The other creatures of the sea became so annoyed with his constant questions that they sent him away to the Great Wise Ones.

"Go down to the deepest, darkest part of the ocean and pester them with your questions!" they said.

So, without hesitation, Carl swam for days and days to the deepest, darkest part of the ocean, in search of one of the Great Wise Ones.

After a long and tiring journey, with weary legs and gills, Carl finally found the home of one of the Great Wise Ones, in a small cave in the deepest, darkest part of the ocean. He was so eager to have his questions answered that he didn't even introduce himself.

"Great Wise One, I have so many questions for you, but the first one I'd like you to answer is this: What are those strange two-footed creatures that walk around on the sand?"

And Polly said, "Oh, I am so glad that you asked!"

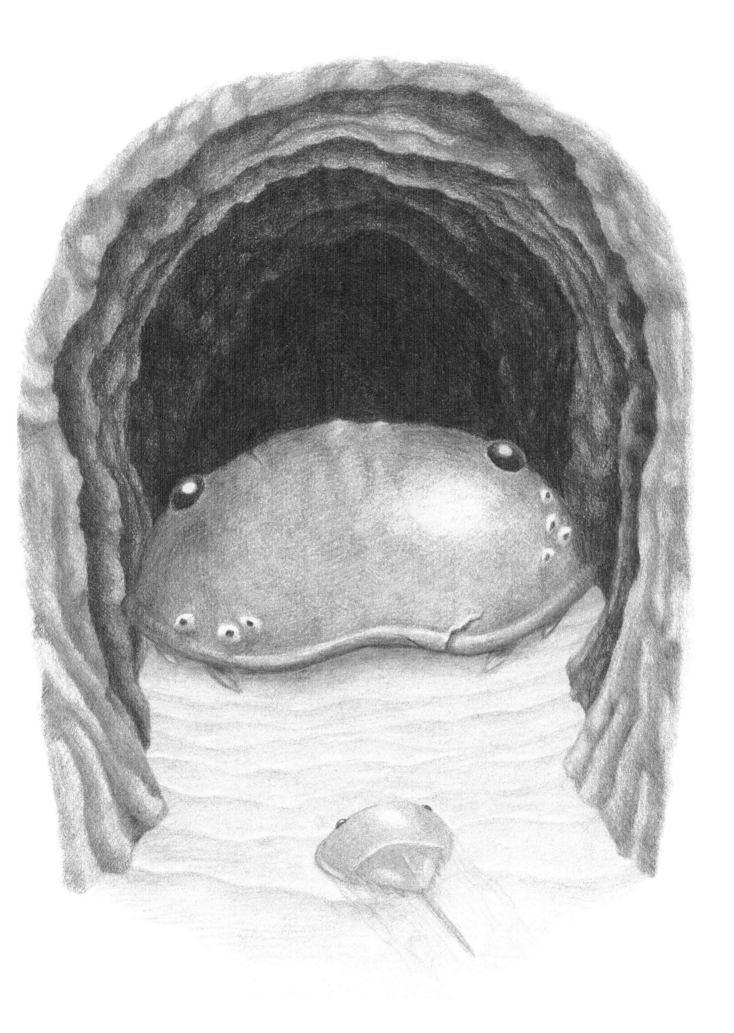

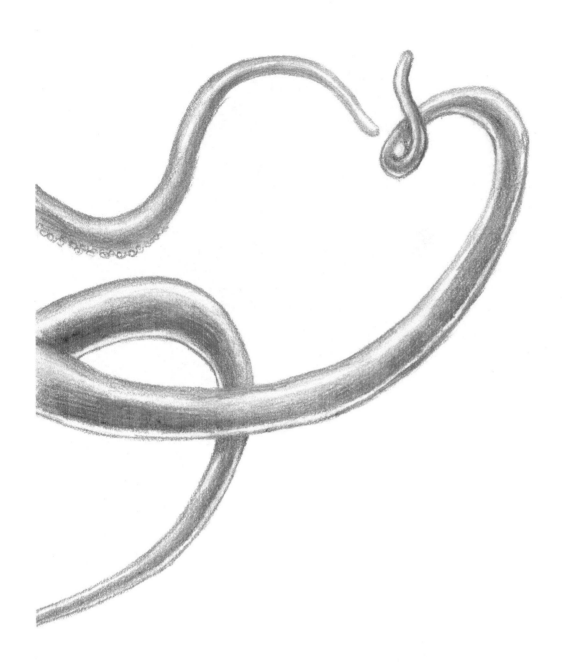

The End

FACTS ABOUT HORSESHOE CRABS

Though she doesn't really know it, Polly is a member of *Limulus polyphemus*, also known by us "Two Feet" as the horseshoe crab. Here are some interesting facts that you may not have known about this fascinating species:

Despite their menacing appearance, the horseshoe crab is completely harmless to humans.

Horseshoe crabs are not actually crabs. They are arthropods, and are more closely related to spiders and scorpions.

The name "horseshoe crab" is thought to have originated from "horsefoot crab," because people thought that their shell resembled a horse's hoof.

There are four known species of horseshoe crabs that exist today. Only one of those four, *Limulus polyphemus*, is found in North America. The other three are found in Southeast Asia.

Fossils of horseshoe crabs date back almost 450 million years—200 million years before dinosaurs existed—and are almost identical to the cr abs that we see today, making them one of the world's most unchanged species.

The tail of a horseshoe crab is called a telson, and it is used to flip themselves over if they become overturned. Picking one up by its telson can hurt the crab, so you should never do this. If you see a horseshoe crab on its back and unable to right itself, you should help it out by flipping it over.

A horseshoe crab's mouth is in the middle of its legs. They feed by bringing food to their mouth using two small appendages called chelicerae, which are in front of the legs. The shoulders of their legs have spiny projections called gnathobases that are used for grinding the food. The family name of the horseshoe crab is *Merastomata*, which literally means "thigh mouth."

Horseshoe crabs have ten eyes. The pair that are easiest to see are mostly used for locating mates. Some of their eyes allow them to see well in the dark, and others are simple light detectors that help the crab know when it is night or day. Some of these eyes are underneath the crab's shell, and some are even located on its telson.

Horseshoe crabs molt their outer covering like other arthropods. As they grow and fill their shell, a new shell grows beneath the old one. Horseshoe crabs walk out of their old shell from a split in the front. Most of the horseshoe crab shells found on the beach are from molting.

Female horseshoe crabs grow to between 16–20 inches long, while the males are a bit smaller at 13–16 inches long.

Female horseshoe crabs can lay almost a million eggs in their lifetime. The eggs are not only important to horseshoe crab population, they are also important to shorebirds, who eat them. In the Delaware Bay alone, shorebirds can eat over 290 metric tons of eggs during a stop on their migratory journey!

Horseshoe crab blood is blue. This is because the blood contains copper that turns blue when exposed to air. It also contains a property that clots in the presence of certain bacteria. This property has been used to develop a test called LAL that is used to confirm the safety of anything injected or inserted in the human body. This test is the gold standard today and has saved thousands, if not millions of lives.

Source: Stacy Epperson, Education Specialist, Maryland Department of Natural Resources.

You can find more books about horseshoe crabs and other sea creatures at your local library. The author read many books about horseshoe crabs while working on this story, including these:

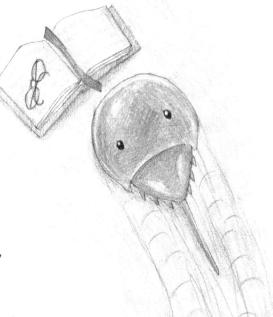

Harry Horseshoe Crab by Suzanne Tate

The Crab From Yesterday by John Frederick Waters

Crab Moon by Ruth Horowitz

Horseshoe Crab: Biography of a Survivor by Anthony D. Fredericks

Horseshoe Crabs and Shorebirds: The Story of a Food Web by Victoria Crenson

The author would like to thank the Two Feet who helped make this book possible through their generous contributions:

a la mode bakery - the Albrights - Alexandria - Stacy & Blake Arnold - Laura Baker - Brad Bean, Jessica Davidson, Elizabeth, Zoe, Meredith, & Ian - Mary Belardo - Susan Schaefer Bernardo - Lilli Blackmore - Jason L Blair - Michael S. Bloss - Maddy V. Born - Bottle of Smoke Press - Nadia Brady - Grimm Brightstave - R. Scott Brittingham - Sharon Buchanan - Steph Burg - the Callicoats - Herman Choi - Arielle & Annemieke deBloois - Joe del Tufo - Kim Dyer - Chris, Beth, Kyler, Kelsea, & Kameron Ferguson - Richard E Flanagan - Pat & Tony Florio - Alex Gaiger - Chris & Tammy Garland - Heather Garritson - Jan Giannetto - the Grant family - Logan Graves - Titia Halfen - Jess Hartley - Morgan Hazel - Julia Ridpath Helvey - Colby and Conner McLelland Ivanosich - Mary Ivanoski - Curly Maple Johnson - Younjin Kim - James Knevitt - Gary A. Knox - the Lambert family - Louise Larsen - Katrina Li - Katharine Magill - Netta Martin - the McCartan Family - Dory McCormick - Amanda Meade - Bob & Kay Meade - Christopher Mennell - Liz and Rick Miller - David Millians - John Moller - Kevin Murphy Jr. - David Nett & Shannon Nelson - Arvin Noel - Wilson Oatley - the Palenchar family - Andrew Pann - Beatriz Parra - Jess Pease & family - Nancy Peralta - Jamie Pierson - Leon Porter Jr. - Aaron Ross Powell - S. ReyBarreau - Edward F. Rishel - Kat & Jason Romero - Abel Rosales - Jenn Rowan - Karen and Chuck Rynkowski - H.L.S. - Ursula Sadiq - Janice Saltsman - Cheryl Holleger Schlitt - the Schmiedlin family - Jesse Scoble - Geoff, Angela & Rhiann Skellams - Cathy Slazinski - Phil, Margaret, and Lorraine Steinhoff - Steve Stutzman - Erin Thomas - Steve Tremblay - Ian Turner - Petra Valentova - Wilfred - Katherine Willham - Nick Wilson - Avonelle Wing - Iryna Yermolayeva

Thank you all for helping make Polly a reality!

-wjw C>-

SPECIAL THANKS

Stacy Epperson (Education Specialist, Maryland Department of Natural Resources); Gary Kreamer (Aquatic Education Coordinator, Delaware Division of Fish and Wildlife); Crayola; Kickstarter; Greg Schauer; J. Denise Baker; Scott A. Smith; Sam Chupp; Wilson Oatley; Jon Anderson; Second Street Players; and my colleagues Bowie, Dio, Hendrix, Reinhardt, Wonder, and Zappa

Along with advice from aquatic specialists, the author used the following resources to help fact-check this book: Fourmilab Switzerland (fourmilab.ch), Google Earth, moonphases.info, and sunrisesunset.com

About the author/illustrator:

Mr. Walton is an artist, musician, writer, performer, and storyteller. He enjoys playing the guitar, banjo, mandolin, bass, and lap dulcimer, drawing, painting sets for plays, acting, telling stories (especially spooky stories), watching old horror and sci-fi movies, playing board games and storytelling games, and appreciating nature. (He has a particular fondness for spiders.)

His favorite things to read are fantasy, horror, and science fiction stories, as well as books on science, mythology, fairy tales, folk tales, and philosophy. His favorite authors are H.P. Lovecraft and Douglas Adams.

Mr. Walton lives in central Delaware with his partner Paula, their two daughters Aylish and Nolah, and a cat named Boris Karloff. This is his first book.

You can find out more about some of the other things Mr. Walton does at www.awkwardlabs.com